A PET FOR MRS. ARBUCKLE

To Barney and Gran
*   and*
Tam and Cindy

Text copyright © 1981 by Gwenda Smyth
Illustrations copyright © 1981 by Ann James
Published in 1984 in the United States by Crown Publishers, Inc.,
One Park Avenue, New York, NY 10016
Originally published in 1981 in Australia by Thomas Nelson Australia
Library of Congress Cataloging in Publication Data
Smyth, Gwenda.
A pet for Mrs. Arbuckle.
Summary: Accompanied by a ginger cat, Mrs.
Arbuckle, who longs for a pet, travels the world over
interviewing exotic animals to find something suitable.
[1. Pets—Fiction. 2. Animals—Fiction. 3. Cats—
Fiction. 4. Travel—Fiction]   I. James, Ann, ill.
II. Title.
PZ7.S66485Pe   1984   [E]   84-1863
ISBN 0-517-55434-8
Printed in Hong Kong by South China Printing Co.
10 9 8 7 6 5 4 3 2 1
First American Edition

A PET FOR MRS. ARBUCKLE

By Gwenda Smyth

Illustrated by Ann James

Crown Publishers, Inc.   New York

Mrs. Emmeline Arbuckle needed a pet.
She needed a pet to look after and talk to.
She had Mr. Arbuckle
but he didn't need much looking after,
and he watched football on TV instead of listening.
Mrs. Arbuckle told the ginger cat from down the street
that she needed a pet.
"Well, of course," said the ginger cat,
"you must advertise."

So Mrs. Arbuckle put an advertisement in the newspaper:
WANTED—A PET FOR A SWEET OLD LADY.
VERY GOOD HOME.

She received eleven letters from animals all over the world.
"Oh, my!" said Mrs. Arbuckle. "Eleven applications!
What happens now?"

"Now you must interview them,"
said the ginger cat.
"I'll come too, in case you need a second opinion."

Mrs. Arbuckle packed her overnight bag
and put on her boots and her shawl.
"We're off," she said—

—and off they went to Mexico to interview an armadillo.

"I'd make a great pet," said the armadillo.
"I could curl myself into a ball
and roll along beside you. Your neighbors would be amazed."

"There's a lot to be said for amazing the neighbors,"
agreed Mrs. Arbuckle.

But the ginger cat said, "Do you want a ball or a pet?
Because if you want a ball, let's go to a toyshop."
"I see what you mean," said Mrs. Arbuckle.

So they said good-bye to the armadillo—

—and went to Africa to interview a giraffe.

Mrs. Arbuckle and the ginger cat climbed up a thorntree
to talk to the giraffe, who was eating the leaves at the top.
"I'd be a stimulating pet," said the giraffe.
"I could see over the fence and tell you
what was happening next door."
"I'd like that," said Mrs. Arbuckle.

"But look at it this way," argued the ginger cat.
"Do you want all the tops of your trees eaten off?"
"No, I suppose not," said Mrs. Arbuckle.

So they said good-bye to the giraffe—

—and went to Patagonia to interview a llama.

The llama came out from the bushes,
and so did his father and mother and sisters and brothers
and aunts and uncles and cousins.

"We're very loving creatures," said the llama,
"and we need a change of scene."
"All of you?" asked Mrs. Arbuckle.
"Oh, I couldn't come without the family," explained the llama.
"What fun to have a yard full of llamas!" cried Mrs. Arbuckle.

"A joke is a joke," said the ginger cat,
"and a pet is a pet, and a herd is a herd."
"You're right, of course," agreed Mrs. Arbuckle.

So they said good-bye to the llama—

—and went to California to see a whale.

"If you took me home," said the whale, "you'd be famous overnight. I'd probably be the first pet whale on the block."

"Oh, what a nice idea!" said Mrs. Arbuckle.

But the ginger cat said, "I suppose you realize
that you'd have to tear down your house
to make room for a pool,
and then where would Mr. Arbuckle watch TV?"
"That *would* be a problem," agreed Mrs. Arbuckle.

So they said good-bye to the whale—

—and flew to Ethiopia to see an aardvark.

The aardvark was poking his tongue into an anthill
and swallowing ants by the hundreds.
"I heard you coming," said the aardvark.
"I can hear things happening far away.
 I could listen for Mr. Arbuckle coming home in the evening
 and tell you when to start dinner."
"That would be helpful," said Mrs. Arbuckle.

"Well *I*," said the ginger cat,
"am not going to spend *my* days finding ants to feed an aardvark.
Are *you* going to spend *your* days finding ants
to feed an aardvark?"
"Maybe not," said Mrs. Arbuckle.

So they said good-bye to the aardvark—

—and went up the Amazon to interview a sloth.

The sloth was hanging upside-down in a rubber tree.
"Will you come down or shall we come up?" asked Mrs. Arbuckle.
"You come up," said the sloth. "I'm clumsy on the ground."

Mrs. Arbuckle climbed up the rubber tree.
"I'd be a pet with a difference," said the sloth.
"You'd get to like me."
"I'm sure I would," said Mrs. Arbuckle.
"There's something about your face."

But the ginger cat said, "You're out of your mind.
What would the neighbors think if they saw
you upside-down in your oak tree?"
"They'd think I was crazy," said Mrs. Arbuckle.

So they said good-bye to the sloth—

—and went to England to interview a frog.

"I have a most unusual voice," said the frog.
"You could lie in bed at night and listen to me croak."
The frog puffed up his throat
and made a very loud noise.
"Goodness!" said Mrs. Arbuckle.
"That *would* be different from listening to the radio!"

But the ginger cat said, "Nonsense!
Pets and people should sleep at night,
and make their noise in the daytime."
"I suppose they should," sighed Mrs. Arbuckle.

So they said good-bye to the frog—

—and went to Canada to meet a grizzly bear.

"Well, here I am," said the grizzly bear.
"You'll never find a pet any furrier."
The grizzly bear looked at Mrs. Arbuckle.
Mrs. Arbuckle looked at the grizzly bear.
"I like your beady little eyes," said Mrs. Arbuckle.

But the ginger cat said, "Take it from me—
bear hugs can be very uncomfortable in hot weather."
"Maybe so," said Mrs. Arbuckle.

So they said good-bye to the grizzly bear—

—and went to Venezuela to talk to a toucan.

"I can carry a lot of fruit in my beak," she said.
"You could send me to the store
  for peaches or pears or plums."
"That would be a help," said Mrs. Arbuckle,
"when Mr. Arbuckle wanted a fruit salad."

"But just suppose," said the ginger cat,
"that she tripped over a cat and swallowed all the fruit!
Then there'd be no fruit salad."
"Mr. Arbuckle *would* be upset," sighed Mrs. Arbuckle.

So they said good-bye to the toucan—

—and went to Tasmania to meet an echidna.

"If you want any digging done, I'm the pet for you,"
said the echidna and he started to dig.
Soil flew up all around him,
and in two minutes he had disappeared into the ground.
"That's a good trick!" cried Mrs. Arbuckle.

But the ginger cat said,
"Who wants holes all over the garden?
Does Mr. Arbuckle want holes all over the garden?"
"Not really," replied Mrs. Arbuckle.

So they said good-bye to the hole in the ground—

—and went to Japan to interview a butterfly.

"I'd be the loveliest pet for miles around," said the butterfly.
"And what's more, you wouldn't have time to get tired of me.
 I only live a couple of days."
"I've *always* loved purple," said Mrs. Arbuckle,
 admiring his wings.

"He wouldn't do at all," snapped the ginger cat.
"A pet should go on and on, day after day.
 A pet should have regular meals
 and sleep in the same old corner night after night.
 A pet should be something you can stroke."
"You're so right," sighed Mrs. Arbuckle, "as always."
 She was sad because there was no one left to interview.

Mrs. Arbuckle and the ginger cat went home.

Mrs. Emmeline Arbuckle made herself a cup of tea.
The ginger cat had a saucer of milk.
"How did it go?" asked Mr. Arbuckle.
"Not well at all," replied Mrs. Arbuckle.
"Not one of the applicants was suitable."
"That's too bad," said Mr. Arbuckle.
He went back to the football game.

"I suppose you'll be going home now,"
 said Mrs. Arbuckle to the ginger cat.
"What home?" asked the ginger cat.
"I don't have a home.
 And I don't dig holes,
 or eat trees, or ants, or plums,
 or hang upside-down,
 or need a pool to swim in.
 And I'm small,
 and soft,
 and *very* smart."

"Well, then, will *you* be my pet?"
 asked Mrs. Arbuckle.
"Oh, yes, yes, yes," said the ginger cat.
"I thought you'd *never* ask."

M090556234

SMYTH, GWENDA

PET FOR MRS. ARBUCKLE.

E MY

E

6/85

CHESTERFIELD COUNTY LIBRARY
ETTRICK-MATOACA

Regular loan: 2 weeks

A daily fine is charged for each overdue book.
Books may be renewed once, unless reserved for
another patron.

A borrower is responsible for books damaged or
lost while charged on his card.

OEMCO